W9-BUC-903

written by
Anne Marie Pace

illustrated by
Frann Preston-Gannon

Busy-Eyed Day

Beach Lane Books
New York London Toronto Sydney New Delhi

Big-eyed bug.

Stalk-eyed slug.

One-eyed Jack.

Two-eyed Zach.

Closed-eyed rider.

Open-eyed slider.

Busy-eyed day at the park.

Weary-eyed
weeper.

Bleary-eyed
sleeper.

Blue-eyed Grammy.

Brown-eyed Sammi.

Blind-eyed
mare.

Cross-eyed bear.

Busy-eyed day at the park.

Eagle-eyed
keeper.

Side-eyed frog.

Round-eyed peeper.

Wide-eyed dog.

Squirrel-eyed girl.

Girl-eyed squirrel.

Busy-eyed day at the park.

Two-eyed skater.

Carp-eyed baiter.

Six eyes?
Eight eyes!

See you later!

No more spiders.
No more bugs.

Loving mama
gives big hugs.

So much to see.
Best place to be . . .

on a busy-eyed day at the park.

For Chuck,
who shares my busy-eyed days—A. M. P.

For Alice Payne,
for all the trees we climbed
and the hours we played—F. P.-G.

BEACH LANE BOOKS • An imprint of Simon & Schuster Children's Publishing Division • 1230 Avenue of the Americas, New York, New York 10020 • For information about special discounts for bulk purchases, please contact Simon & Schuster Special Sales at 1-866-506-1949 or business@simonandschuster.com. • The Simon & Schuster Speakers Bureau can bring authors to your live event. For more information or to book an event, contact the Simon & Schuster Speakers Bureau at 1-866-248-3049 or visit our website at www.simonspeakers.com. • Book design by Lauren Rille • The text for this book was set in Archer. • The illustrations for this book were rendered using a mixture of both digital and hand-drawn techniques.
Manufactured in China
0118 SCP
First Edition
10 9 8 7 6 5 4 3 2 1
CIP data for this book is available from the Library of Congress.
ISBN 978-1-4814-5903-7 (hardcover)
ISBN 978-1-4814-5904-4 (eBook)